GHOST DETECTORS
Curses!

BOOK 10

BY
DOTTI ENDERLE

ILLUSTRATED BY
HOWARD MCWILLIAM

magic
Wagon

visit us at www.abdopublishing.com

A big thank you to Adrienne Enderle — DE
With thanks to my ever-supportive wife Rebecca — HM

Printed in the United States of America
052011
092011
 This book contains at least 10% recycled materials.

Text by Dotti Enderle
Illustrations by Howard McWilliam
Edited by Stephanie Hedlund and Rochelle Baltzer
Cover and interior design by Jaime Martens

Library of Congress Cataloging-in-Publication Data

Enderle, Dotti, 1954-
  Curses! / by Dotti Enderle ; illustrated by Howard McWilliam.
    p. cm. -- (Ghost Detectors ; bk. 10)
  ISBN 978-1-61641-626-3
  [1. Mummies--Fiction. 2. Blessing and cursing--Fiction. 3. Ghosts-
-Fiction. 4. Humorous stories.] I. McWilliam, Howard, 1977- ill. II.
Title.
  PZ7.E69645Cu 2011
  [Fic]--dc22
                        2011001842

Contents

What's Spooked Spooky?

Malcolm and Dandy sat in the basement lab, sorting through a heap of mail. Because Malcolm subscribed to zillions of weird magazines, it sometimes took a while to sift through to the good stuff. Three had arrived today. They were *Beastly Beings, Absurd Serpents,* and Malcolm's favorite, *Ghostly Gallows.* Lots of ghost-hunting tips in that one.

Sandwiched between the magazines was a glossy ad addressed to "Resident."

Malcolm unfolded it, smiled, then handed it to Dandy. "Check this out!"

The Museum of Natural Science presents

THE TOMB OF TUTURTIKUM

Buried 3,000 years ago, the mummy of Egyptian Pharaoh Tuturtikum will be on display along with many of the splendid treasures found within his ancient tomb.

View emeralds that shimmer like the Nile! Sapphires that gleam like the Egyptian sky! And diamonds that twinkle like forgotten stars!

Come marvel at Tuturtikum and his riches on exhibit all month. Open Daily 10:00 to 6:00

Dandy's face split into a grin. "This is great! When can we go?"

"Are you kidding? We're going this weekend!" Malcolm cheered. He reached over and powered up his specter detector so his phantom dog, Spooky, could play.

Yip! Yip! Spooky was small and see-through, but he had the energy of a rocket

ship. He bounced up and down, biting at Malcolm's sleeve. Malcolm snatched up a tennis ball and rolled it across the floor for Spooky to fetch. Of course, Spooky could never grab it. But trying to retrieve it kept him busy for five minutes or more.

"I think we should get to the museum the second it opens," Dandy said. "I want to be first in line."

Malcolm couldn't agree more. "Just think, we're among the lucky people who get to see the actual mummy of Tuturtikum."

Dandy flipped the ad over to the back. "Here's his picture."

"Before or after they mummified him?" Malcolm asked.

"After." Dandy held it up for Malcolm to see. "He's gray and stiff and kind of raggedy."

"Just like Grandma Eunice," Malcolm teased.

"Except Tuturtikum is 3,000 years old," Dandy added.

Malcolm smiled. "Just like Grandma Eunice."

Yip! Yip! Malcolm could see Spooky's frustration at not being able to grip the ball.

"Here you go," Malcolm said, leaning over and grabbing it. Spooky followed, sniffing his hand. "Fetch!" He rolled it hard this time. The ball wheeled across the floor, bounced off the wall, and went right through Spooky.

"The exhibit starts this Saturday," Malcolm told Dandy. "We'll need to get there early."

Dandy's face lit up. "Hey! Maybe we should camp out on Friday night!"

Malcolm picked up the ball again, causing Spooky to bounce like a runaway spring. "I don't think that's a good idea."

"Sure it is," Dandy said. "We can pitch our sleeping bags on top of that big sundial in front of the museum. That way we won't be late."

"Uh, Dandy, I don't think the sundial has an alarm on it. And it's sort of slanted, so I kind of think we'd both roll off. We could end up with more bandages than Tuturtikum."

Malcolm set the ball rolling again. "We'll just have to meet super early to get in line."

Dandy flipped the ad over, then held it high, trying to get Spooky to jump for it. But Spooky backed away, snarling.

Grrrrrrr.

Malcolm leaned toward him. "What's the matter, boy?"

Dandy reached over, holding the ad.

Grrrrrr! Spooky backed farther away. *Grrrrrr!*

Malcolm looked at Dandy. "What are you doing to him?"

"Nothing," Dandy said. "Maybe he doesn't like glossy paper."

Malcolm shook his head. "He sometimes lays on my magazines. They're glossy."

"Maybe he doesn't like the colors," Dandy suggested.

"That's silly," Malcolm said. Then he looked at the ad. "Maybe he doesn't like the picture." He motioned for Dandy to hold it out. Spooky shot across the

THE TOMB OF TUTURTIKUM

basement and hid behind a cabinet, out of sight.

"Why would this ad scare him?" Malcolm wondered.

Dandy shrugged. "Maybe Tuturtikum hated dogs."

"But why would that matter to Spooky?" Malcolm asked. "Tuturtikum is long dead and sealed away at the museum. And Spooky is right here."

"Hmmm . . . We don't know how old Spooky is," Dandy said. "Maybe 3,000 years ago Spooky belonged to Tuturtikum."

Malcolm shook his head. "I don't think so."

Dandy looked back at the ad and shrugged. "Well, I'm out of ideas."

But Malcolm barely heard Dandy. His wheels were turning. Why would Spooky be afraid of a museum ad?

"You know what, Dandy?" Malcolm asked. "I think there's something the museum isn't telling us about Tuturtikum."

Dandy's eyes grew wide. "Really? What do you think they're hiding?"

Malcolm turned on his computer. "I'm about to find out."

Dandy scootched over next to him.

Malcolm opened a search engine and typed in *Tuturtikum*. The first thing to pop up was his tour. "Wow, this guy is like a rock star!"

"Yeah, he even has his own fan page," Dandy pointed out. "Look at the photos. People actually show up wrapped like mummies."

Malcolm nodded. "They look like you did on Halloween."

"Only it looks like they used bandages instead of toilet paper."

Malcolm didn't care about the fan page. It was the link below that caught his attention.

"Uh, Dandy. I think I know what spooked Spooky." He clicked on it. The page banner read: *The Tuturtikum Curse!*

The Tuturtikum Curse

"Whoa!" Dandy piped. "There's a curse? A real curse?"

Malcolm scrolled down the page. "Yeah. Here's an article about it." Dandy leaned in as Malcolm read.

After twelve years of digging in the sizzling Egyptian heat, Professor Cecil Cell and his crew have discovered the long-lost tomb of Tuturtikum. King Tikum, as he is known, was one of Egypt's most feared Pharaohs. Historians have named him the Crueler Ruler.

His subjects slept in pigsties while he slept in palaces. They ate garbage while he ate grapes. His clothes were tailored while theirs were tattered. The people meant nothing to him. He only cared about his riches and his queen, Neferatissue, who wore a white lotus flower in her hair instead of a crown.

The wealthy Tikum stored all his gold and jewels in a pyramid that would one day be his crypt. He visited the site daily to roll around in his mountain of coins. No one dared try to rob him. No one dared come close. The king had proclaimed that anyone who touched his riches would be cursed forever, even after his death.

Years and years of agony continued as Tuturtikum treated his subjects as slaves. The commoners became fed up with this treatment and soon plotted a way to get rid of their king.

The annual Festival of the Ferret had arrived. Every year, King Tikum would open the ceremony

by charging down the main street in his chariot shouting, "Long live me!" But this year the people were ready for him. Workers made a fat, stiff mud brick, placed it along the parade route, then waited.

Depicted here in hieroglyphs, King Tikum lashed through at great speed. His chariot hit the mud brick, sending the Pharaoh flying up, up, up in the air. He bounced off a festival banner, hit a fig tree, then landed in a wine barrel placed strategically on a steep hill. The barrel tipped over and rolled down the hill at such great speed even Queen Neferatissue couldn't catch it. It whirled and twirled until finally dropping into the opening of Tuturtikum's tomb. The barrel, with Tikum inside, crashed into the statue of a laughing jackal. Tikum was gone for good.

The queen, happy to be rid of her rotten husband, removed the lotus flower from her hair, pitched it into the tomb, then partied through

the night with a handsome nobleman and an assortment of weaselly ferrets.

Professor Cell and his crew removed King Tikum and his treasures shortly after their discovery. Among the items was an ancient slate. Upon it was written:

Anyone who dare disturb this tomb shall be triple cursed.

You shall swim with piranhas!

Be afflicted by an itchy pox!

And face the Horrendously Dreadful Thunder Beast!

Ignoring the curse, they sent the contents to the British Museum. Then one by one, they fell victim to Tikum's curse.

Just weeks later, Cell's assistant fell into a puddle of piranhas while working near the Amazon.

At the same time, the digging manager contracted a severe case of chicken pox.

And Professor Cell, himself, disappeared into a bottomless cave. People nearby claimed to hear only his pleas for help and the thunderous roar of some unknown beast.

Tuturtikum's mummy has traveled from place to place since 1972. Many have fallen victim to his curse, but only those who are brave enough to stare his cobra in the eye.

Dandy stared, mouth gaping. "His cobra?"

"I think they mean this." Malcolm pointed to a photo of the mummy. On top of his black, shriveled face was a blue-and-silver headdress.

Dandy bit at his lower lip. "I thought that was just a fancy towel."

"No, it's a Pharaoh hat. They all looked

like fancy towels. And that gold Cobra is what's holding it on his head."

Dandy studied the photo. "It's hard to tell from this picture, but it looks like that snake has red eyes."

Malcolm nodded. "They must be made out of rubies."

"Who cares?" Dandy said. "I'm not about to get close enough to see! I have enough problems without getting cursed."

"Yeah," Malcolm agreed. "We can look at everything else at the exhibit, just don't look at that cobra."

"No problem," Dandy said.

Doomed!

Malcolm was up bright and early on Saturday morning, antsy to get to the museum. Unfortunately, his parents had decided to go, too. Yikes! A family outing? So much for being the first in line.

"Why do I have to go?" Cocoa whined as Mom and Dad shuffled everyone toward the door. "I hate filthy old dead things!"

Malcolm pointed to her furry, rat-gray knee boots. "Then why don't you give

those a proper burial? Or are you wearing them to make your feet smell better?"

Cocoa gave him the stink eye. "I'm going to cram one of them down your throat if you don't shut up."

"Enough," Mom warned. "Cocoa, this is a once-in-a-lifetime opportunity."

Cocoa crossed her arms and pouted. "Why would anyone want to line up for a decrepit old geezer that looks like a month-old pickle that's been left out in the sun?"

"For a date!" Grandma Eunice exclaimed as she wheeled by.

"Grandma, this guy's been dead for 3,000 years," Malcolm pointed out.

"Good," she said. "He can't get away."

"Let's just go," Dad huffed.

Malcolm met Dandy at the entrance. They stormed through the door and up the steps only to wind up at the end of a long line that stretched past the butterfly exhibit. It went behind the antique ketchup jar collection and under the skeleton of T. Bones, the museum's terrifying T. Rex.

"We're going to be here all day!" Malcolm complained.

Beep! Beep! Grandma Eunice wheeled ahead, beeping everyone aside with a bicycle horn attached to her wheelchair.

Dandy watched her zoom off. "Think we could hitch a ride?" he asked Malcolm.

That's when Malcolm noticed Cocoa near the front. She'd cut in line with some of her friends. "No fair!" he griped. "She didn't even want to come here!"

Malcolm bent down and peered through T. Bone's bony legs so that he could get a better look at the exhibit entrance. The pyramid-style door had large, leafy fronds fanning the opening. Above it were hieroglyphs of the sun and moon, a cat wearing an Egyptian kilt, and a man with a dog head holding a giant eye.

Malcolm had no idea what it meant, but the dog and cat appeared to be dancing. Maybe the eye was some type of mirrored disco ball.

Malcolm could also see the exit—a simple doorway. People walked away with looks of amazement. "It must be fantastic," he told Dandy.

After what seemed like a decade, but was only twenty minutes, they finally entered.

"Look at all this!" Malcolm said to Dandy. But Dandy was too wowed to answer.

The room shimmered among the glow of Tuturtikum's treasures. Jewels and trinkets piled so high they sparkled like the glitter in Dandy's fancy gel toothpaste.

"Check this out," Dandy said, pointing to a large urn labeled *Canopic Jar*. "What's a c-c-canopic jar?" he asked.

Malcolm read the label next to it. "It says it's a vessel that contains human organs. I guess they're his."

Dandy made a sour face. "Ew. You think his gizzard's in there?"

Malcolm nodded. "Definitely."

They moved a little farther into the exhibit. "Hey, look at this!" Malcolm said,

pointing to a cluster of stones carved like bugs. "The sign says they're scarabs."

Dandy leaned as far over the railings as he could. "Scarabs? They look like cockroaches to me."

Malcolm read out loud, "These charms are in the form of the scarab, a type of dung beetle. They were sacred to the ancient Egyptians."

"They look like something my mom would squash with her shoe."

Malcolm and Dandy were awed at some of the stuff Tuturtikum had stored away. Mummified cats – *"Cool!"* – funeral masks – *"Trick or treat!"* – and a pair of wooden sandals – *"Wouldn't you get splinters in your toes?"*

Finally they reached the main attraction—old Tuturtikum himself.

"I didn't know that mummies were so dark and crumbly," Malcolm said.

"Yeah, he sort of looks like a licorice skeleton wound up in filthy rags," Dandy pointed out. "But look, he's still wearing his snake hat. Don't stare at it."

Malcolm glanced up. The mummy was propped up next to his sarcophagus, a fancy word for coffin. Malcolm could see the cobra on top of King Tikum's head, but it was much too high to look in the eye.

"Don't worry," he told Dandy, "we're safe."

But just then something extraordinary happened. A museum worker opened the back of the display to adjust a toppled vase. Being a bit klutzy, he accidentally hit the sarcophagus. It swayed a little to the left, tilting Tuturtikum forward.

The worker quickly righted the king
before he fell flat on his creepy face. But
not in time to stop Malcolm and Dandy
from catching a peek at the cobra's ruby
eyes.

Malcolm blinked. "Did that just
happen?"

Dandy stood stiff, his eyes like ping-
pong balls. "Oh no! We're doomed!"

Piranhas!

"What are we going to do?" Dandy asked frantically as he and Malcolm stood outside by the museum's fishpond.

"Maybe it's nothing," Malcolm suggested. "Maybe we just imagined it."

Dandy danced a frenzied shuffle. "We didn't! Did you see that glare? It was like a laser! Or Mrs. Goolsby's death stare!"

"It was intense," Malcolm agreed.

Dandy added some hand-wringing to his shuffle. "Let's face it, Malcolm, we've been zapped with an ancient curse."

Malcolm was shaky, too, but didn't want to admit it. "Come on, it can't be that bad. A curse? Really? No one believes in those things."

"I do," Dandy whined. "I've seen it before."

"When?" Malcolm asked.

Dandy leaned closer as though saying it too loud would bring down the wrath. "My aunt Belinda. She walked under a ladder on Friday the 13th."

"Did anything happen?" Malcolm asked.

"She tripped over a black cat and broke a mirror."

"Then what happened?" Malcolm wondered.

"It was raining and she couldn't get her umbrella open. She tugged and tugged, then gave up. As she walked into a restaurant, the umbrella popped up. Scared her so bad she backed into a table and spilled a whole shaker of salt. A waiter cleaned it up before she had a chance to throw some over her left shoulder."

"Is your aunt okay?" Malcolm asked.

Dandy shrugged. "I don't know. We haven't seen her in a while. She's afraid to leave her house."

"Dandy, those are superstitions, not curses. The Tuturtikum Curse doesn't exist. It was something made up to sell tickets to the exhibit." He wanted to assure his friend, but he really wasn't so sure himself.

"You're sure we're not headed for disaster?"

"I'm sure," Malcolm said. "Now let's go check out the snack bar. Did you see the names of some of those soft drinks? Pyramid Punch. Mummy Mango. Sphinx Fizz."

"Yeah," Dandy agreed. "Being struck by an ancient curse makes you awfully thirsty. And I think I'll get the Sphinx—" *Beep!*

Malcolm and Dandy hadn't seen Grandma Eunice zooming toward them. The sound of her horn startled Dandy right out of his sneakers and – *splash!* – into the fishpond.

"Help! Help! Piranhas!" he cried. "The curse is real! Piranhas! I'll be eaten alive!" Dandy pushed and paddled, trying to swim to safety. "Help!"

"Now that's a sight," Grandma Eunice said as she wheeled closer. "Get out of there, silly, you're scaring the goldfish."

"But I can't swim!" Dandy gurgled.

"You don't have to," Grandma said. "There's only two feet of water in that pond."

Dandy stopped splashing and stood up. The water came up to his knees. He waded out, his clothes stuck to him like jelly.

"Still think there's no curse?" he whispered to Malcolm.

"If there was a curse, the water would've been ten feet deep, not two, and the goldfish would've had razor-sharp teeth," Malcolm pointed out.

"Well, I could've hit my head," Dandy argued.

"But you didn't," Malcolm countered.

"I could've broken my arm."

"Didn't happen."

"I could've choked on a goldfish."

Malcolm tilted his head and gave Dandy a look. "None of those things happened."

Dandy sat down and slipped his sneakers back on. "Let's go to the snack bar."

"Woo-hoo! Refreshments!" Grandma cheered as she zipped her wheelchair around in a circle. "My treat!" *Beep! Beep!*

Malcolm leaned toward Dandy and murmured, "See. Grandma's paying. There is no curse."

Dandy sloshed along, leaving a drippy trail. "No curse? I'm a walking puddle. No way they'll let me back inside."

33

We All Scream for Ice Cream

Malcolm and Dandy sat at a picnic table in a nearby park.

"I think my underwear shrunk," Dandy complained, tugging at the seat of his pants.

"I can't believe you thought those goldfish were piranhas," Malcolm said.

Dandy shivered. "They were fishy and scaly with bulging killer eyes and razor-

sharp teeth! They could've ripped me apart!"

Malcolm wasn't sure if it was the wet clothes or the thought of killer goldfish that caused Dandy to shiver. Or maybe it was the idea of them being under an actual curse.

"First of all," Malcolm began, "you can't even see goldfish teeth. I think they're microscopic. Practically invisible."

"Then maybe it was the water making them look a thousand times bigger," Dandy admitted, pulling on the seat of his pants again.

"Second of all," Malcolm continued, "there is no curse. Falling into that pond was an accident."

Dandy leaned forward and a trickle of water slid down his face. "Okay. Falling

into that pond was an accident. Not getting back into the museum was bad luck. My underwear shrinking to the size of a mitten was *a curse*! And don't get me started on missing out on the snack bar."

That was true. Malcolm felt a little cheated about not getting his Sphinx Fizz. "Hey," he said, trying to cheer Dandy up.

"Think about it. I stared at the cobra's eyes, too, and nothing happened to me. See?" He spread his arms to show that he was curse-free.

"Are you sure you looked it in its eyes?" Dandy asked, swiping another dribble of water from his face. "Maybe you blinked."

Malcolm thought a moment. "I saw them," he said. "They were like two red-hot coals burning into my eyeballs."

"That's what I saw, too!" Dandy said.

"But it could've just been a reflection," Malcolm told him.

Dandy raised an eyebrow. "A reflection of what?"

"You know," Malcolm stalled, "like when the sun reflects off a magnifying glass. That's blinding. It could have definitely been a reflection."

Dandy raised both eyebrows. "Or it could've been the rays of an ancient Egyptian curse choosing its next victims."

Malcolm shook his head. "Whatever."

It was right then that Malcolm heard the sweet sound of the ice cream man.

"See?" Malcolm beamed. "We're not cursed. Got any money?"

Dandy pulled at his pocket, which was water-sealed to his pants, and dug out some coins.

"Oh, great," he said. "I had two dollars. I think they must've washed out into the pond. Now they're fish food." He slumped forward, resting his chin on this hand. "I'm definitely cursed."

"But putting money into a fishpond is good luck," Malcolm countered. "Didn't you see all the coins at the bottom?"

"I wasn't looking at the bottom," Dandy said. "I was looking at a school of piranhas that were planning to eat me as the main dish."

"They were goldfish, Dandy."

"But they looked hungry." Dandy yanked at the seat of his pants and grimaced. "I feel like I'm wrapped in cellophane."

"Hey," Malcolm said, wanting to cheer him up, "I have some extra money. Let's get some ice cream."

They hurried over to where the ice cream truck was parked. Malcolm looked over the flavors. "What do you want?" he asked Dandy.

Dandy looked like he was struggling to decide, too. The ice cream man, who looked a little like Santa Claus, tapped his fingers.

"I can't make up my mind," Dandy told Malcolm. "I like everything."

"I know," Malcolm agreed. "But I want something chocolate."

"Ooooh! Chocolate and banana," Dandy said. His mouth might have been watering, but it was hard to tell.

The ice cream man drummed his fingers some more. "Come on, I haven't got all day."

For an ice cream man, he isn't very jolly, Malcolm thought.

Dandy was still scanning the choices. "I bet it's fun driving an ice cream truck, huh?" he asked the man.

"Are you kidding?" the ice cream man snarled. "It's a curse!"

Malcolm and Dandy flinched.

"I drive around all day," the guy complained. "I don't make much money. And I have to listen to this stupid song for hours and hours. I've practically ground my teeth down to nubs. One day I'm going to get a baseball bat and crater that scratchy speaker. And if I hear 'Pop Goes the Weasel' one more time, I'll go insane! Now, what flavor would you like?"

Malcolm gulped as he said, "A chocolate cream stick."

"I'll have a-a-a cherry ice pop," Dandy stuttered.

The man opened the small freezer door and pulled them out. "That's two dollars," he said.

Malcolm was just about to hand over the money when – *whoosh!* – it blew out

of his hand and danced across the parking lot.

"Catch it!" Malcolm yelled, racing for it.

Dandy waddled in his wet clothes, trying to keep up with Malcolm. Malcolm chased after the money as it rose and dipped, blowing in different directions. He weaved around cars, signs, and speed bumps as the cash led them on. The money sailed up over a tree and finally floated into a patch of weeds near a field at the dead-end street.

"It's under these bushes," Malcolm said, dropping down on his hands and knees.

"Let me help," Dandy offered.

They crawled under the prickly brush and felt around.

"I know it's in here," Malcolm said, plucking away some vines.

Dandy pulled in closer. "Is that it over there?"

Malcolm saw them a few feet from his grasp. The dollars were camouflaged within the thick leaves.

"Got 'em!" he shouted, feeling victorious. He waved the two bucks in the air. "One chocolate cream stick and one cherry ice pop coming up!"

The boys darted back to the parking lot just as the ice cream man pulled away and puttered off down the road, "Pop Goes the Weasel" fading into the distance.

Dandy slumped, hung his head, and tugged at the seat of his pants. "Curses!" he whined.

The Pox!

Malcolm woke up the next day feeling like he'd swam in a tub of hot sauce. His face and arms were on fire. He wanted to scratch, but he wasn't sure where to begin.

He crept out of bed, trying not to touch anything. Even the soft sheets felt like a grater shredding his flesh. That's when he looked down. *Ahhhhh!* His arms were covered in huge red blisters and sores! He rushed over to the mirror and – *Yikes!* – so was his face!

"The pox! The pox!" he yelled.

Then the phone rang. Malcolm picked it up and heard Dandy screaming, "The pox! The pox! It's real! The curse is real! I have the pox!"

Malcolm clawed his itchy arm. "I have it, too."

Dandy was silent for a moment, then, "It's real! It's real!" he screamed again.

"Listen," Malcolm said, trying to talk over Dandy's hysteria. "We'll figure something out."

"Tuturtikum's pox is upon us," Dandy whined. "We'll slowly rot and decay until we look just like him."

"We won't rot," Malcolm assured him. "I'll think of something."

"Think of it quick," Dandy said. "I've nearly clawed my skin off."

Malcolm knew the feeling. "King Tikum won't get us," he assured. "But I've got to hang up now. Grandma Eunice has a drawer full of fungus cream, and I may have to fight her for it."

When Malcolm walked into the kitchen, his mom's jaw suddenly dropped. "Oh my goodness!" she cried.

Malcolm had scratched his face so much it felt like he'd been slapped with a whiffle bat about three dozen times!

Mom hurried over to examine the rash. "This looks awful."

Cocoa stumbled in about that time. "Hey! Did you fall asleep under my sunlamp?"

"Your sunlamp couldn't burn a flea," he argued. "And besides, why would I want to crawl under something that you've decorated with pink kitty stickers?"

"Alright," Mom said calmly. "Enough of that."

Malcolm lightly scratched his nose. He didn't want Cocoa to know how badly it itched.

Then Grandma Eunice rolled in. "Whoopsie!" she exclaimed. "Looks like somebody's been cursed with the pox."

"What?" Malcolm said, trying to control the panic in his voice. "I have the pox?"

Grandma winked. "Naw, just kidding. But that's a bad case of poison ivy you've got there."

Malcolm breathed a sigh of relief. "I have poison ivy?"

"Yes," Mom said. "Don't touch anything."

"What should I do?" he asked her.

"Soak in the tub for a bit, then we'll apply some calamine lotion."

Grandma clacked her dentures and said, "And don't go sneaking through my drawer of fungus cream."

The Dreadful
Thunder Beast

Malcolm and Dandy sat in the basement lab trying their best not to scratch. They were slathered in calamine lotion, making their skin the same color as Cocoa's pink kitty stickers. The specter detector was on, and Spooky cowered in the corner.

"What's wrong with him?" Dandy asked. "He hasn't yelped a single yip."

"Yeah, I think he senses something," Malcolm said. "He doesn't want to come close."

Dandy took a sniff of his arm. "Maybe it's because we smell like dog soap."

Malcolm nodded. "Or maybe because we look like the Colossal Lobsters from Outer Space."

Dandy patted the floor. "Here, Spooky. Come on, boy."

Spooky backed into the corner so far his tail disappeared into the wall. *Grrrrr!*

"I think I know what Spooky's afraid of," Dandy offered.

"What?" Malcolm asked.

Dandy lowered his voice to a whisper. "It's the curse."

Malcolm sighed. "Dandy, how can you still believe there's a curse?"

"I swam with piranhas," he said.

"Goldfish," Malcolm corrected.

"I have the pox," he argued, holding his arms out like Frankenstein's monster.

"It's not the pox," Malcolm said. "It's poison ivy." The mere mention of the name had Malcolm wanting to scratch.

Dandy cocked an eyebrow. "That's just it," he said, still in whisper mode. "How did we get poison ivy? We were at a museum. There's no poison ivy at a museum."

Then Malcolm remembered. "The money! We chased it into those bushes. Those bills were caught in the ivy underneath."

"Oh great!" Dandy said. "We missed out on ice cream and ended up with a prickly rash. It sure feels like a curse to me."

"Don't worry," Malcolm assured him, "it's not a curse."

Then suddenly – *Boom!* – they heard a earsplitting crash of thunder. It scared Spooky so much he faded into the wall.

Malcolm's heart skipped a beat or two. "What was that?"

Dandy's eyes bugged. "Sounds like a bad storm."

Malcolm walked over to the window and peeked out. The sky was an amazing blue with a bright, shining sun. "It's not a storm."

Boom! Hugging his knees to his chest, Dandy said, "I think it's coming from inside the house!"

Malcolm tiptoed to the stairs.

Dandy stood up and crept over by him. "Is anyone home?" he asked Malcolm.

Malcolm shook his head. "No. Mom and Dad took Grandma Eunice to visit a friend. And Cocoa snuck out to visit her boyfriend."

"Cocoa has a boyfriend?" Dandy asked, looking confused.

"A miracle, huh?" Malcolm said. "And he's just as goofy as she is."

"Hard to believe," Dandy snickered.

Boom! They both jumped, knocking into each other.

"Ah!" Dandy shouted. "Malcolm, remember the last part of the curse? It's him. It's the Horrendously Dreadful Thunder Beast!"

"It's probably nothing," Malcolm assured him.

"It doesn't sound like nothing," Dandy said.

True. Malcolm knew something was up there, and it wasn't Cocoa singing or Grandma Eunice dribbling her autographed Harlem Globetrotters basketball. "Maybe we should check it out."

"Go ahead," Dandy said. "I'll wait here so Spooky won't be all alone."

Malcolm looked at the wall. The ghostly dog was hiding inside. Only his nose was sticking out, sniffing the air. "I think Spooky will be fine." Then Malcolm picked up a soda bottle to use as a club, gazed up the stairs, and said, "Let's go."

Dandy grabbed onto the sleeve of Malcolm's T-shirt and held tight. Slowly

they crept up – step, stop, step, stop, step. *Boom!*

Dandy squeezed the sleeve tighter and whispered, "It's near the door."

Malcolm nodded. "Don't worry. It can't hear us. We'll catch it by surprise."

Step, stop, step, stop, step. They'd made it to the top.

Malcolm looked at Dandy and mouthed, "Ready?"

Dandy shook his head no.

Malcolm reached for the handle anyway, held it just for a second or two, then flung it open!

Roaaaaarrrrrrr!

A blast of hot, dusty wind hit them hard! They screamed and stumbled their way down the stairs.

"Malcolm, is that what I think it is?" Dandy asked, bypassing Malcolm's sleeve and clawing into his arm.

Malcolm quivered so hard he could barely nod yes. "It's him!"

Filling the doorway with his was evil presence stood the rotting corpse of Tuturtikum!

Say Cheese!

*R*oaaaaarrrrrrr!

Malcolm pinched his nose closed. "Dude, your breath smells like last week's fried chicken!"

Dandy turned a sickly shade of green, and Malcolm didn't know if it was from fear or King Tikum's breath. "Hit him!" Dandy finally shouted.

Malcolm raised the soda bottle high. "He's not close enough."

"Throw it at him!" Dandy insisted.

"I can't." Malcolm held the bottle toward Dandy. "You throw it."

"I can't throw it. My hand is cramped from clutching your sleeve!"

Boom! Tikum took a step closer. He leaned forward, took a dive toward the steps, then flew upward and off through the ceiling. *Roaaaaarrrrrrr!*

Malcolm dropped the bottle as he and Dandy gripped the stair rail to keep from falling.

"Whoa!" Dandy shouted. "It was him! The curse is real! He's after us!"

Spooky slipped out from his hiding place in the wall. That meant the coast was clear.

"I'm not so sure," Malcolm told Dandy.

"Not sure? Didn't you see him? It was a mummy!"

"I don't think so," Malcolm said. He walked over and turned off his specter detector. Spooky vanished with one final *Yip!*

"Well, if it wasn't Tuturtikum's mummy then what was it?" Dandy asked frantically.

Malcolm gave Dandy a stern look. "It was Tuturtikum's ghost."

Dandy turned a much paler shade of green. Combined with the rash and calamine lotion he now looked like an inflated pufferfish.

"What are we going to do?" Dandy asked.

Malcolm snatched up the specter detector and aimed it toward the ceiling.

"We're going back to the museum."

They arrived at the entrance a little before six. There was no hustle and bustle or long lines this late on Sunday.

The girl at the counter gave them a worried look. "Are you contagious?" she asked, careful not to touch them when she handed over their tickets.

Malcolm smile innocently. "No. It's just poison ivy. You can't spread it."

She cowered back. "Okay, but please don't touch the exhibits."

"No problem," Malcolm said, hoisting his backpack higher up on his shoulder.

They hurried over to Tuturtikum's display. Only a few stragglers remained.

"We're closing shortly," a large security guard informed them. Malcolm had seen big men before, but this guy looked like a refrigerator with a badge.

"We'll look fast," Dandy said.

The guard stared. Then, he nodded and stepped back.

Malcolm and Dandy strolled in front of the display, pretending to ooh and aah over all the trinkets. They were pretty cool. Tuturtikum may have been a selfish guy, but he had excellent taste in treasure.

Finally the other visitors stepped out. Malcolm unzipped his backpack.

"Hey!" the guard called. "It's closing time."

Malcolm pulled out the specter detector. "Just let me take a quick picture."

"That's one goofy-looking camera," the guard said.

"It's a new model," Malcolm told him. It wasn't a lie. Malcolm had bought the

brand new version of the Ecto-Handheld-Automatic-Heat-Sensitive-Laser-Enhanced Specter Detector.

"Well, no photos," the guard warned.

Malcolm didn't listen. He aimed the specter detector straight at Tuturtikum's crumbly mummy and powered it on.

"Say cheese!"

Armored Insects

"What in the world!" the guard screamed as Tuturtikum's ghost stepped out of his mummified body. "Is this some kind of trick?"

The words had barely left his mouth when the ghost huffed a deep breath and – *Roaaaarrrrrrr!* – knocked the guard backward out of the room. Then with a *wham! wham! wham!* the doors slammed tight, locking him out.

"Hey!" the guard hollered as he pounded on the door.

"That guard isn't going to be too happy when we come out," Dandy said as Malcolm handed the detector over to him.

Malcolm pulled out the ghost zapper. "Let's worry about that once we make it out."

Tikum stood in front of them with his arms crossed mummy-style.

"Oh, you're just asking for it," Malcolm said. He pressed the button a little too late. The ghost did a backflip over the rails and landed near his sarcophagus.

"I've got plenty of juice in here," Malcolm warned him. "I'm not going to stop until you're dethroned!" He aimed again, but before he could press the button, he felt something scurry around his ankles.

"Bugs!" Dandy yelled, dancing around a large army of scarabs that had come to life, dropped down off the exhibit, and was clicking around their feet.

Malcolm shuffled back but it was no use. Those bugs were crawling everywhere. Over his shoes, his socks, and finally, up his pants!

"No!" he screamed. He twisted and shook as the rigid little creatures climbed higher and higher.

"What do we do?" Dandy asked, kicking and hopping.

Malcolm put down the zapper. "We've got to get them off of us!"

Malcolm tried tramping them, but there were too many. He tried brushing them away with his foot. They just kept coming. Then he looked over. Dandy had

stripped off his pants and was squirming around in his underwear and socks.

"Ahhhh!!!" a half-naked Dandy yelled. He skipped over as many beetles as he could and jumped over the rails and onto the exhibit stage. "Help!"

Malcolm raced toward it too, *crunch, crunch, crunch*. He leaped onto the exhibit with Dandy.

"They're everywhere!" he said, watching the beetles skitter across the floor.

"Except up here," Dandy pointed out. "I think we're safe."

"Really?" a voice behind them croaked.

Malcolm and Dandy froze. The ancient, dusty breath of King Tikum tickled Malcolm's neck. They both turned.

"Forget something?" Tikum asked, pointing to the ghost zapper lying on the floor, covered in scarabs.

Drat! Malcolm couldn't believe it. How could he have been so stupid as to forget the zapper? It's amazing the silly things you'll do when you're being bombarded by beetles.

Malcolm put on a brave face—unlike Dandy's, which was now the color of crusty custard. "You can't win, Tikum," Malcolm challenged.

The ghostly mummy grinned. "Looks like I've won already. You'll be stuck in here with me forever."

Forever? Won't the museum people bust down the door, exterminate the insects with bug bombs, pack Tuturtikum's mummy in a crate, and ship it off to the next city? Maybe not.

Dandy stood, shivering. "I don't want to be stuck here forever. Not without my pants."

Tikum let out a frightening laugh. "Maybe we could find something to wrap you in," he said, nodding toward the decaying linen strips that wound around the mummy.

Malcolm kept one eye on Tikum, the other on the zapper. He had to find a way to grab it without being swarmed by scarabs.

"So what are we going to do?" Dandy asked.

Before Malcolm could answer, the ghost of Tuturtikum dropped down in front of them. "You're going to be my slaves," the evil Tikum threatened.

"Never!" Malcolm said, leaping off the stage and jogging toward the zapper. The crackle of crunching beetles didn't stop him. He snatched up the zapper and—

"Not so fast," the ghost bellowed.

Oh no! The ruby-eyed cobra had come to life. It hissed and slithered and crawled . . . up and around Dandy's feet.

Hiss!

"Uh, Malcolm," Dandy squeaked. "Could you maybe zap the cobra?"

"I don't think so," he said. "It's not a ghost. But whatever you do, don't look at its eyes!"

The cobra rose up, spreading its hood.

"It's about to strike!" Dandy cried. "Help!"

Tuturtikum slipped up behind Dandy. "I control the serpent," he told Malcolm.

"So put that weapon down or your friend gets it."

Malcolm had two choices. Put the zapper down, or charge forward, hoping to make the rescue before the snake sank its fangs into Dandy's scrawny leg. But then, Malcolm saw another option.

"Malcolm!" Dandy trilled as the snake reared back.

Just before it could spring forward, Malcolm snapped up Dandy's pants and flung them like a sail. They landed on top of the cobra with a *puff!*

"Run, Dandy!" Malcolm shouted, hopping over beetles to join him.

Dandy scrambled in the wrong direction. He darted toward the center of the exhibit, and Tikum's mummy.

The ghost blasted a breath of wind, sending Dandy flying into the sarcophagus. And with a *bam!* the coffin slammed shut.

Malcolm whipped the zapper toward Tikum, but the tricky ghost disappeared.

"Dandy!" he cried, trying to open the sarcophagus. "Can you hear me?"

"Yeah," Dandy said, sounding amazingly calm.

"Can you breathe?" Malcolm asked.

"Yeah. But I'm trying not to. Do you know what a 3,000-year-old mummy's coffin smells like?"

"Pretty bad, huh?" Malcolm said, trying to find some kind of latch. "I'm going to get you out."

"Can you do it soon?" Dandy asked. "My poison ivy itches and I can't reach it."

Malcolm pulled and pried. Nothing. "It won't open," he told Dandy.

"I'm going to be stuck here forever," Dandy said. "Would you do me a favor, Malcolm?"

"What?" Malcolm asked as he looked around for something to wedge into the coffin door.

Dandy let out a tiny sob. "Tell my mom that I love her. Tell my dad that I didn't mean to break his 'Perfect Game' bowling trophy. And tell Mrs. Goolsby she was right, I did copy off Sarah Tingler's math test last Thursday."

"You can tell them," Malcolm said, trying to encourage his friend.

If only he could zap Tuturtikum. That would solve everything. But you can't zap a ghost that you can't see. There had to be

some way to draw him out. That's when a light came on in Malcolm's brain. What did the stingy old pharaoh love most?

"I'll be right back," Malcolm told Dandy.

He wasted no time gathering up Tikum's jewels. He crammed emeralds in his pockets, wrapped gold pendants around his neck, and was just about to slip on a diamond ring when—

"What do you think you're doing?" the ghost bellowed.

Malcolm shrugged. "I figured you can't use them. I could probably get a lot of money for this stuff. You know, buy some new ghost-hunting equipment. Maybe a pool for the backyard. I could even send my great-grandmother on one of those senior cruises where they play shuffleboard and bingo and—"

"No!" he roared. "Those are mine!"

The ghost charged toward Malcolm, flying at great speed. But not fast enough. Malcolm drew up the ghost zapper and sprayed him. Tikum melted mid-air into a shimmery puddle, then evaporated.

"Dandy!" Malcolm yelled, rushing back to the sarcophagus. The door easily swung open. There stood Dandy, eyes closed, arms crossed like a mummy. Malcolm shook him. "Are you okay?"

Dandy opened one eye. "Is he gone?"

Malcolm nodded. "We're no longer cursed."

Dandy eyed the jewelry Malcolm was wearing. "Not a good look for you."

No Reward

The boys trudged back into Malcolm's house and down to the basement lab. Luckily, Dandy was wearing pants.

"Another ghost gone," Malcolm said, feeling proud.

"Yeah," Dandy agreed. "The museum people should give us an award."

"Dandy, we sort of messed up their exhibit. I don't think they'd reward us for that. Besides, they didn't know about

the ghost or the curse. They have no clue what we did."

Once Tuturtikum had turned to goo, Malcolm and Dandy had found a back entrance and slipped out.

"We wipe out ghosts all the time," Dandy pointed out. "And no one even pats us on the back."

Malcolm powered up the ghost detector. "Here, Spooky," he called.

Spooky peeked out of the wall, afraid to come closer.

"It's okay," Malcolm said, grabbing the museum ad and ripping it into colorful flakes.

Yip! Yip! Spooky danced out, his see-through tail wagging.

"Good boy," Malcolm said, running his hand through Spooky's pointy ears.

"At least Spooky is grateful," Malcolm said.

Dandy knelt down to pet the dog, too. "Guess it's over," he said.

"Yeah," Malcolm agreed. "I just hope the museum folks get the exhibit back in order and—"

"Move it off to the next town," Dandy finished. He ran his fingers over Spooky's

tail. "So do you think the curse has been lifted?"

Suddenly a fierce howling resounded through the house. Dandy nearly jumped into Malcolm's arms. "What's that?"

Malcolm covered his ears. "It's Cocoa practicing her choir solo."

"Are you sure that's not someone torturing a cat?"

"Not unless a tortured cat can wail out 'Hello Dolly.'"

Hellooooooooooooo, Dolly! Wah, wah, wah! Dolly!

"Wow, that could make your head explode," Dandy said.

Malcolm leaned back and sighed. "Yeah. Looks like I'll always be cursed."

TOOLS OF THE TRADE: FIVE USES FOR THE GHOST DETECTOR

From Ghost Detectors Malcolm and Dandy

1. Use it as a prop for Halloween when you dress as a space cowboy or alien hunter.

2. Leave it on in your room as a night-light.

3. Give it to your best friend to hold so he can't run away screaming.

4. Detect a ghost that is hurting people or animals in order to make the community a safer place.

5. Fool adults into thinking you are just playing with a toy when you are actually doing important work that will keep them safe from angry spirits and their curses!